Now Cow Helps Drama Llama

A Mindful Tale for Coping with Anxiety

by Kelly Caleb

Illustrations by John Van Hout III

Dedication

For David and Tiara, I wish I had Now Cow to help me be more mindful when you were little

Thank you to Liz, Nicole, Jen - my office daughter, Mike and Kendra (My Iowa writers), and for the many friends and family that encouraged me and made this happen!

Library of Congress Control Number 2019917610.
ISBN: 978-1-7333783-0-7

Now Cow Helps Drama Llama:
A Mindful Tale for Coping with Anxiety

Kelly Caleb
Illustrations by John Van Hout III
- 1st Edition

Drama Llama ran through the herd,

trampling flowers to spread the word.

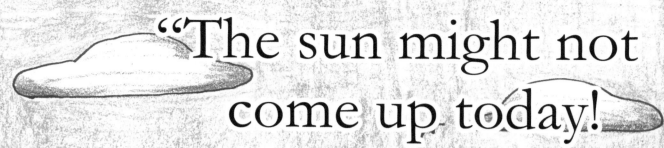

"Drama Llama, you worry so.

The sun will rise, this I know."

Now Cow breathed in, and then breathed out,

walked a bit and did not shout.

"Drama Llama, cold or hot,
enjoy the day and walk alot.
Feel the grass beneath your feet.
Taste the hay and chew the wheat".

The sun could fall
out of the sky!

If it does, well, we'd all die".

Now Cow was basking in the sun
and had no plans to up and run.

"Drama Llama, what will you do
if the sun should fall on you?

You worry this. You worry that.
You see less clearly than a bat.

Calm the voices in your head.
They only fill you up with dread".

Drama Llama plopped in a heap,
a heaping heap of self defeat.

"Yesterday was a bad day.
The worst-est worst in every way.

Tomorrow will be dreadful too.
The dread-est dread
for me and you".

Now Cow perked up a brow at this
but kept all thoughts on inner bliss.

"Drama Llama, can you not see?
The worst of your catastrophe

is in your mind.
It's in your head from when you rise
'til you're in bed. Just let it go.

Breathe in. Breathe out.
There is no need to rush about.

The sun will rise. The sun will set.
This simple thing you do not get.

You cannot gain control and power.
You cannot force one single hour

to go faster through time and space
by worrying about its pace.

Breathe in. Breathe out.
Enjoy the day and maybe
you will find your way

to peace and calm and happiness.
Try some thoughts of inner bliss".

Drama Llama looked away.
"I do not like a word you say.

For if I do not rush about,
and if I do not yell and shout,

then others will not know I'm here.
I'm afraid I'll disappear".

Now Cow chewed and thought on this,
this lonely llama with no bliss.

"Drama Llama, have no fear,
for you will not disappear.

You are not here because of me.
I am not here because of thee.

You do not need to rush about.
You do not need to yell and shout.

The grass is silent every day,
yet still it grows and still it stays.

Perhaps it knows a thing or two,
something more than me or you.

As it rises from the earth,
it worries not about its worth.

It simply is. So simply be.
Just be you. I'll just be me".

Drama Llama thought on this,
this mindful cow full of bliss.

"Now Cow, I will try your way
of being for a single day.

I will breathe in and then breathe out.
I will not rush or yell or shout.

I will watch the flowers grow
and not give in to

fear of rain,

fear of snow,

or fear of doom.

I will give myself some room
to find out who I am today,
to think on things a peaceful way".

And so they sat side by side, shaggy fur and spotted hide,

breathing in and breathing out without a rush or yell or shout.

Peacefulness was found that day,
on the hillside full of hay.

And, if you're wondering what
it's all about, first breathe in and
then breathe out...

Na-moo-ste

CPSIA information can be obtained
at www.ICGtesting.com
Printed in the USA
LVHW071009020320
648688LV00011B/352